one mitten

Clarion Books
a Houghton Mifflin Company imprint
215 Park Avenue South, New York, NY 10003

The illustrations were executed in acrylic gouache.
The text was set in 20-point Italia Book.

www.houghtonmifflinbooks.com

Printed in China

Library of Congress Cataloging-in-Publication Data

George, Kristine O'Connell.
One mitten / by Kristine O'Connell George ; illustrated by Maggie Smith.
p. cm.
Summary: One mitten can do many things, but when the second mitten is found, it is time to go outside and have fun.
ISBN 0-618-11756-3
[1. Mittens—Fiction. 2. Lost and found possessions—Fiction. 3. Stories in rhyme.]
I. Smith, Maggie, ill. II. Title.
PZ8.3.G2937One 2004
[E]—dc22 2004000135

ISBN-13: 978-0-618-11756-7
ISBN-10: 0-618-11756-3

SCP 10 9 8 7 6 5 4 3 2 1

one mitten

by Kristine O'Connell George • Illustrated by Maggie Smith

Clarion Books / New York

One mitten,
yellow and bright,
fits on my left hand . . .

or on my right.

One mitten can wave
a mitten hello.

PIGS

One mitten can make
a shadow show . . .

with shadow shapes
of a mitten whale

and a slow, slow
mitten snail.

One mitten is a hat
for a rooster's head,

or a very small
mitten-bag bed.

One mitten
is a mitten flag.

"Hold still, Daisy . . ."

"Wag, Daisy, wag!"

One mitten gives my sleepy cat
a kitten-soft one-mitten pat.

And, under the cat, some yellow fuzz . . .

My other mitten!

So that's
where it was!

Two mittens can clap,

flap mitten wings,

make mitten ears—

lots of
two-mitten things.

Two mittens windshield-wipe
the frosty glass.

It's snowing outside,
covering up the grass!

Two mittens make binocular eyes.

Two mittens wave
mitten goodbyes.

Then, one mitten,
yellow and bright,
holds my friend's hand
warm and tight.

Two friends with mittens,
we're ready to go—

skipping, mitten-warm,
into the snow.

For the Colorado cousins
—K. O. G.

For Zoë and Isobel
—M. S.